Plant Facts and

Sylvia Woo

Illustrated by Yvonne Skargon

ff

faber and faber

LONDON · BOSTON

First published in 1985
by Faber and Faber Limited
3 Queen Square London WC1N 3AU

Filmset by Wilmaset, Birkenhead, Merseyside
Printed in Great Britain by
Redwood Burn Ltd., Trowbridge, Wiltshire

British Library Cataloguing in Publication Data

Woods, Sylvia
Plant facts and fancies.
1. Plant—Juvenile literature
I. Title
581   QK49

ISBN 0–571–13436–x

Contents

Introduction

From earliest times, plants have played an important part in people's lives. In the Bible story, Adam and Eve were created in a garden and set to work in it, and men and women have been gardeners ever since. For centuries before the coming of modern drugs, people depended on the healing properties of plants for their health and well-being. Plants have always provided food and given their fragrance to make perfume. Apart from their usefulness, flowers are so beautiful that they have been grown and loved for themselves alone. Over the years, stories, traditions and superstitions have grown up about them. This book gives an account of some of the plant lore which has come down to us through the centuries.

1

Nature's Clocks and Plants for the Traveller

In the past, country people used to manage without clocks and calendars. They told the time and marked the passing of the seasons by studying plants. If you wear a digital watch and like to time events in hundredths of seconds, you certainly wouldn't be satisfied with the countryman's less accurate methods. You might also notice that British Summer Time upsets the timing of Nature's clocks because it puts all man-made clocks forward an hour during the summer months.

In more leisurely days, twelve o'clock or mid-day was reckoned as the time when the sun was at its highest in the sky in our hemisphere. Country people rose with the sun, worked until the mid-day rest and then went back to their labours until sunset. They noticed that some flowers seemed to have their own built-in clocks which caused them to open and close their petals at the same time each day.

They called goat's beard 'Jack-go to bed at noon' because it closed its petals towards mid-day. To make up for such early retirement, it was also an early riser, opening at four o'clock each morning. Goat's beard flowers in early summer and is found in fields and hedgerows throughout Britain, except in the very north of Scotland. Its flowers are a cheerful yellow and it is easily seen because it grows about 60 centimetres high. It keeps faithfully to its opening and closing times, which may be useful if you aren't wearing a watch. But remember, goat's beard knows nothing about British Summer Time!

The lovely orange flower which we call marigold is called

calendula by gardeners, to distinguish it from tagetes, which is used for the French, Mexican and African marigolds. It opens its petals when the sun rises and closes them as it sets. Shakespeare wrote about this flower in *The Winter's Tale*:

> *The marigold, that goes to bed wi' the sun*
> *And with him rises weeping.*

The marigold looks a very jolly flower and it is difficult to imagine why it should weep. Probably Shakespeare was thinking of the dewdrops on the petals, which dry out as the sun reaches them.

The Star of Bethlehem is a garden plant in this country, but it sometimes grows wild where it has escaped from gardens. It has the country name of 'the eleven o'clock lady' because it opens its flowers around eleven o'clock in the morning. If the weather is dull, however, the flowers may not open at all. It has large white flowers which grow in clusters and is a very attractive plant. There is another Star of Bethlehem, a smaller plant which grows wild in the woods. Its tiny yellow flowers really do look like stars on the woodland floor. They open early each morning, but by mid-day they have closed again and the pointed green buds are all that one sees until the following morning.

If you have evening primroses in your garden, go out in the evening just as the light is beginning to fade and watch the flowers unfold. You can actually see the petals move, slowly at first, then the flower pops open and the stalk is covered with pale fluttering petals which shimmer in the dark. Once these flowers grow in your garden, you will always have them, because they seed very easily. As the old plants die down, there are always half a dozen or more seedlings to take their place.

These flowers are all time-keepers and could be called the countryman's clocks. There is one flower which acts as both clock and barometer. The scarlet pimpernel is often called the 'poor man's weatherglass'. A weatherglass is better known

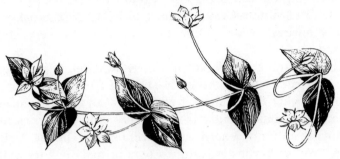

scarlet pimpernel

nowadays as a barometer, which is an instrument which records atmospheric pressure, so it can forecast changes in the weather. The scarlet pimpernel, a tiny low-growing plant found in fields and on waste ground, opens its neat pointed scarlet petals early in the morning around seven o'clock and closes them an hour or so after mid-day. If rain happens to be on the way after the flower has opened its petals, it will close up at once, and the observant passer-by is warned that there is going to be a change in the weather. On dull days, the flower usually remains closed all day, so what with closing its petals after mid-day and not opening at all when the sun doesn't shine, the scarlet pimpernel is not a very satisfactory flower from the point of view of helping you to be your own Weather Man.

People who don't want to invest in a barometer may prefer to rely on a piece of seaweed. The broad ribbon type is best, because it is very sensitive to humidity in the atmosphere. Before it actually rains, the seaweed absorbs the dampness in the air around it and becomes soft and wet, warning you that rain is on the way.

For a really long-range forecast, most of us remember the rhyme about the oak and the ash.

> *Ash before oak, sure to be a soak,*
> *Oak before ash, only be a splash.*

Plant Facts and Fancies

By studying the unfolding oak and ash leaves, we can foretell the kind of summer we are going to have. As the oak tree is nearly always in leaf before the ash, this is a very popular rhyme.

The long-range forecast for winter weather is provided by another pair of trees, the holly and the hawthorn. There is a popular belief that if these trees have a lot of blossom in the spring and consequently bear a heavy crop of berries in the following autumn, a hard winter will follow. The idea is that a large crop of berries is Nature's way of making sure that the birds will have plenty to feed on in bad weather. It is an unscientific way of looking at things, but it might be interesting to keep a record of bumper crops of berries to see if a hard winter does follow.

Once the winter is here, we look forward once more to signs of spring and the warmer weather. There can be false hopes, of course, and just as we are warned that 'one swallow does not make a summer', north country people say that one daisy does not make it springtime. There is a saying in the north of England that spring has not arrived until you can place your foot on twelve daisies. The Old English name for daisy was 'day's eye', because its petals opened at dawn and closed at dusk. If you have daisies on your lawn at home, you can test the truth of this.

Snowdrops are called 'fair maids of February', because this is the month of the year when most of them are at their best. In sheltered spots, they bloom in January, but February is the month when they grow tall enough to hang their heavy white heads tipped with green above their spear-like leaves.

Lady's smock is a delicate mauve flower of a shade so pale that the dark pink veins can easily be traced on each petal. It grows along miles of hedgerow all over Britain and sometimes in fields and woods as well. Country people call it the 'cuckoo flower', because it blooms at the time when the first cuckoos are heard, which is in April.

Nature's Clocks and Plants for the Traveller

In the Middle Ages the crocus was associated with St. Valentine's Day, because it was supposed to bloom at dawn on 14th February, but today there are many varieties of crocus which flower at different times during the spring. Besides, since the Middle Ages there has been a change in our calendar. In 1752 the Gregorian Calendar with its system of leap years was adopted in Britain. This method of dating had been used by most European countries since the sixteenth century and Britain was eleven days behind by its reckoning. The last day of the old calendar in our country was fixed for Wednesday September 2nd. The next day was put forward eleven days and became Thursday September 14th.

The Gardener's Calendar

There is a great deal of folklore connected with the times we are supposed to plant our crops. The traditions vary in different parts of the country. St. Valentine's Day is said in the south to be the right date for the first sowing of onions, garden peas, sweet peas, lettuces and cabbages. Scotsmen in their cooler climate wait for the first swallows to arrive before they begin planting. Gardeners who want to make sure of missing the late frosts of early summer wait for the mulberry tree to bear its leaves before sowing their seeds. Mulberry leaves are very easily killed off by frost and the leaves of this tree tend to appear later than those of others. This piece of advice is very old. The Roman writer Pliny the Elder mentioned it in his treatise on natural history in A.D. 77. As there are very few mulberry trees growing in our gardens today, the gardener has to rely on long-range weather forecasts from the Meteorological Office.

Another Roman writer, the poet Virgil, wrote a long poem called the *Georgics* which is really a book on agriculture (the title comes from the Greek word for 'farmer'). He had his own farm in the region of Campagna near Naples. He told farmers to watch the cluster of stars known as the Pleiades, these stars should have disappeared from the autumn skies before any winter crops are sown.

In the West Country there is a saying,

> *When you hear the cuckoo shout*
> *'Tis time to plant your tatties out.*

Most gardeners, however, plant their 'tatties' or potatoes on Good Friday, regardless of the cuckoo. This is one of the best known of all planting traditions. The actual date of Good Friday varies from year to year because the date of Easter is governed by the phases of the moon, but it so happens that almost every Good Friday comes at a time when the moon is waning. There was a strong belief, dating back to pagan times, that all root crops should be planted on the wane for good results.

In the nineteenth century it was the custom for a farmer to lend ploughs and horses to his labourers on Good Friday so that they could prepare and plant their own potato plots. After morning service, the day was a holiday, so the farmers felt that they lost nothing by parting with their horses and ploughs, and their labourers spent their holiday planting potatoes.

While the men attended to the heavy work of potato planting, women would be busy in the herb garden on Good Friday sowing parsley. An old Christian tradition says that it should be sown during the hours of twelve o'clock and three o'clock, the time of the Crucifixion. It is a plant which germinates slowly and one reason given for this is that it has to return seven times to the devil before it can come up in our gardens.

Plants for the Traveller

Before the coming of the motor car, life was lived at a much more leisurely pace. Although the wealthy travelled in horse-drawn vehicles or rode on horseback, the majority of people walked from place to place. If you were one of those foot travellers, you could count on certain plants to help you on your way.

mugwort

Mugwort was supposed to possess magical powers and writers of ancient Rome recommended every traveller to carry a sprig of it. It was said that he who travelled with this plant on his person would never become weary. It sounds rather a far-fetched claim. Some authorities think that mugwort is a corruption of 'midgewort', which might mean that wearing a sprig of midgewort keeps midges away. Mugwort is a common plant, found growing in hedges and on waste land. Its leaves are green on top and have white undersides. It flowers from July to September.

Lady's bedstraw has a more practical use than mugwort. It used to be steeped in water and the liquid was used to bathe sore feet. Not only travellers benefited. In the seventeenth century it was recommended for lackeys, footmen and other servants who were constantly on their feet during the course of their work.

Distilled water of hawthorn flowers was strongly recommended for any unfortunate traveller who had a thorn or splinter in his foot. Before the thorn was extracted, the part of the foot where it had entered was bathed in the liquid. The thorn or splinter would loosen and could be pulled out more easily.

Traveller's joy is another name for the wild clematis which grows in our hedgerows. It is a climber, scrambling all over other plants in the hedge, covering them with clusters of green

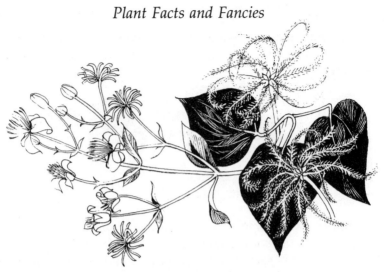

traveller's joy

and white flowers from May to June. Later these flowers turn to seedheads full of grey tufted seed vessels which have earned it the name of 'old man's beard'. The Elizabethan herbalist John Gerard described it in his *Herbal*, which was a book giving the history and description of all plants and trees known to the Elizabethans. In his day the plant was called viorna, but this didn't please John Gerard. He wrote about the way it had of 'decking and adorning the waies and hedges where people travel; and thereupon,' he adds, 'I have named it the Traveller's Joy.'

Gerard liked finding new names for plants, and he was especially fond of a tree which grew on the chalk downs to the south of London, on the Pilgrim's Way. This was the road which pilgrims had once taken from London to Canterbury. There were no pilgrims in Gerard's day but the road was still used by ordinary travellers and wayfarers, so in his *Herbal* he called the tree the wayfaring tree, which is the name we still use today.

The pretty little low-growing flower of the germander

18

speedwell with its bright blue petals was believed to do just what its name says. It sped travellers on their way and kept them safe on their journeys. Some travellers in the past had such faith in the speedwell that they had the plants sewn into their clothes before setting out.

Fast travellers like runners and messengers were advised by the ancient Greeks and Romans to put chamomile or artemisia in their shoes to prevent their legs from getting tired. It does not seem very practical advice. More useful was the idea of using chamomile flowers in a hot bath to relax the body after strenuous exercise.

Some people think that the Madonna lily was first brought to Britain by the Romans. The juice from the lily was said to cure corns, which the soldiers developed on their long route-marches.

prickly lettuce

The prickly lettuce is the traveller's compass plant. It is a tall, stiff, wild lettuce which grows up to 70 centimetres high. It has prickles on the underside of its leaves and along the mid-rib, and many of the leaves have stiff bristles along their edges. It is not a very common plant in this country, but it can be found. The leaves twist themselves about, sometimes growing out

19

horizontally from the stem and sometimes standing almost upright. When the sun shines, the leaves are supposed to twist so that the tips of the leaves which grow up the stem on alternate sides point due north and south. The traveller has to look at the sun to decide which leaves are pointing north and which south, otherwise he may end up very far from his destination, and regret placing so much trust in plants.

2

Helpful Plants and Good Companions

Centuries ago, farmers and gardeners in many parts of the world discovered that certain plants, grown alongside others, would help produce a healthy crop of fruit or vegetables. They thought that these plants possessed a special kind of magic and must be sacred plants provided by the gods who watched over the harvest.

Today, scientists and nurserymen have discovered that some plants actually do give off chemical secretions which enable other plants near them to grow more healthily. In some cases, the chemicals feed the plants, in others, the chemicals enter the soil and kill off various pests which attack crops.

As far as we know, the farmers of ancient Ecuador and Peru were the first people to discover the beneficial effects of tagetes on their vegetable crops. There are three major varieties of tagetes, known as French, African and Mexican marigolds. These early South American farmers grew sweet corn, potatoes, beans and tomatoes on irrigated terraces cut out of the mountain slopes where they lived. The roots of these vegetables were often attacked by eelworm and when this happened the harvest was poor. The farmers discovered that where the Mexican marigold had seeded itself, there were always good crops because the roots were not attacked by eelworm.

In the 1960s, a Dutch bulb-grower made an interesting discovery. He started to grow another type of tagetes, the African marigold. When his bulbs had finished for the season,

African marigold

he found the African marigolds made a good cut-flower crop which he could sell in the flower markets through the summer. Some years his bulbs used to be badly attacked by eelworm, but he noticed that where tagetes had been grown, they remained healthy and immune from eelworm attack. Scientific investigation showed that the roots of tagetes gave off a special secretion which killed eelworm. So the 'magical' properties of tagetes had been explained by twentieth century science. There are now many brands of chemical sprays and powders available for pest control, but tagetes is still used by many nurserymen to prevent eelworm attack on all sorts of crops from beans to strawberries.

Many of us consider stinging nettles a nuisance, but gardeners have learnt to appreciate them as a source of fertilizer for their crops. Early farmers noticed the effect of nettles and thought that they must have magical powers. Today we understand more accurately how the nettle works its 'magic'. As it grows, it takes all sorts of nutrients from the soil and stores them up. It retains chemicals like nitrogen, phosphate, protein, iron, silica and other solid salts. When nettles are made into a fertilizer, all this goodness is given back to the soil, enriching it and making it possible to grow better crops.

In a recipe used in the sixteenth century, and possibly earlier, nettles were cut just before flowering and placed in a wooden cask. This was filled with rainwater and the nettles were left to ferment in it for a month. Then what was left was diluted with ten parts of rainwater and sprayed on the ground. This recipe is just as effective today as it was then. It is a good way of making use of all those nettles you have in the garden, but leave a few to grow in an odd corner, because butterflies like the Peacock and the Red Admiral like to lay their eggs on the leaves.

a butterfly on a nettle

Market gardeners have found that tomatoes, plums, nectarines and peaches tend to stay fresher for longer if they are packed among nettle leaves when they are sent to the main fruit and vegetable markets throughout the country.

There are other ways of keeping the produce fresh. Some people say that apples are best stored between layers of maple leaves. Many North American fruit-growers think that each type of fruit should be packed in its own leaves to keep it fresh while travelling.

Rhubarb leaves also are useful to gardeners. Long ago, they found that if the leaves were left for a few weeks in rainwater, they made a liquid which would kill many types of insect which attack the leaves of fruit trees. We know today that rhubarb leaves contain oxalic acid, but the old gardeners didn't know that. To them, it was magic.

Another old remedy used rhubarb stalks. Short lengths of stalk were placed in holes made for planting cabbages. Where this was done, the cabbages flourished, because the oxalic acid, working its 'magic' again, prevented club-root from attacking the plants.

Garlic, chives and onions have been used for centuries to keep pests away from crops. The leaves of wild garlic, when boiled in water, make an effective pesticide, and garlic planted among raspberry canes and close to vines seems to keep away pests which attack these plants. If boiling water is poured on to a basin of chives, the liquid can be used to dab on gooseberry leaves to prevent mildew. Onions are often sown between rows of carrots to prevent carrot pests. There is an old Dorset tradition of planting an onion beside a rose bush to make the rose smell sweeter. Bulgarian farmers, who grow roses on a large scale to make the perfume known as attar of roses, have always believed that planting onions or garlic among their roses makes their perfume stronger.

There seems to be no scientific explanation for the use of these plants to ward off pests. Perhaps their strong smell keeps harmful creatures away. As to why the roses smell sweeter for having an onion as a companion, maybe the answer is that when the rose bush is free of pests it produces better-scented flowers.

You might think that the tomato has too strong a smell to make a good companion plant, but it is just this strong smell which is so useful. Some gardeners hang old tomato plants on fruit trees to keep pests away. Years ago, the Indians of Mexico used old tomato plants in their houses to keep cockroaches away.

The elder tree has a long history of helpfulness in the garden. Cottagers used to hang branches of elder over fruit trees and cabbage plants to keep harmful insects away. Elder twigs were stuck in the ground along rows of broad beans to discourage blackfly, and there is a story of a New England gardener who used to whip the trunks of his apple tree with young elder branches to keep insects away.

This use of elder trees is all part of the magic of tree lore which is described in Chapter 8. There does not seem to be any scientific reason for it.

Herbs have always provided a border for the cottage vegetable garden. Their pungent smells are thought to keep insect pests away. Good companions among the herbs include borage, lavender, thyme and lovage, and these herbs are all useful in cooking or providing perfumes.

An exception to these companionable herbs is fennel. There is a country saying which goes:

> *Sow fennel,*
> *Sow trouble.*

But fennel is useful in fish dishes, and all herb gardens seem to include it, so gardeners can't find it all that much trouble. The fennel plant does grow very big, and takes up light and air from other plants, so perhaps that is what the old saying means.

The seventeenth century herbalist William Coles wrote:

'among strawberries sow here and there some borage seed and you shall find the strawberries under those leaves far larger than their fellows.' Strawberries themselves are supposed to be good companions. The Tudor gardener Thomas Tusser wrote in 1557:

> *The gooseberry, respis (raspberry) and rose all three*
> *With strawberries under them trimly agree.*

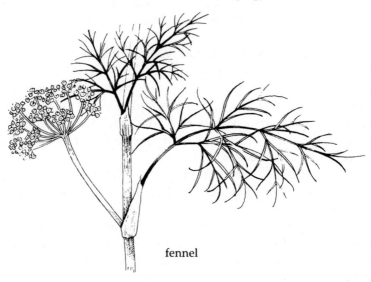

fennel

3

Medicinal Plants

In the Middle Ages and as late as the seventeenth century, plants were in great demand as cures for illness, and most men who practised as doctors possessed a thorough knowledge of their healing properties.

Some of these men had their own large gardens where they cultivated herbs. One of the most famous of these 'gardening doctors' was the Elizabethan surgeon, John Gerard. He had a garden where he grew his own herbs in Fetter Lane, Holborn. This kind of garden was called a 'Physick garden' in those days, and Gerard grew over a thousand different kinds of herbs, many of which came from abroad.

He was born in Cheshire and in 1562 was apprenticed to a surgeon. For twenty years he practised his profession, but he was also superintendent of Lord Burleigh's gardens in the Strand. When Elizabeth I died and King James I came to the throne, he made Gerard his own doctor.

In the Middle Ages, the men who were usually the best doctors were monks. There were monasteries all over the country and they all had herb gardens. The monk in charge of the monastery herb garden was called the Infirmarian or Farmerer, and he looked after the monks who were ill. He knew a lot about the healing properties of plants and made up his own medicines, and he would train a younger monk, who took his place when he died.

27

Plant Facts and Fancies

Herbs and Astrology

Curing people by herbal remedies was a very complicated process, which began long before the patient actually received his medicine. Doctors believed that herbs worked properly only if they were planted and gathered at the right time of the day, month and year. Dry herbs, for example, had to be gathered when the moon was waxing. At that time they were thought to have less sap in their leaves and stems. Roots, on the other hand, had to be gathered when the moon was waning, because they were then at their tenderest.

Herbalists also had to take note of the twelve constellations in the Zodiac, which is an imaginary zone in the sky inside which the planets travel. This area is divided into twelve equal spaces which are governed by twelve star signs: Aries, Taurus, Gemini, Cancer, Leo, Virgo, Libra, Scorpio, Sagittarius, Capricorn, Aquarius and Pisces. Each star sign covers a different part of the year, as you will find if you 'read your stars' in the daily newspaper. There was a strong belief that both plants and humans are affected by the star signs under which they were born, so a patient's stars had to be studied, as well as his aches and pains, when herbal remedies were prescribed. One herbalist wrote:

> 'Gather all leaves in the hour of the planet that governs them . . . let them be ripe when they are gathered and forget not the celestial harmony before mentioned, for I have found by experience that their virtues are twice as great at such times as others.'

This extract comes from the *Herbal* of Nicholas Culpeper, who was one of the last astrologer-herbalists to practise in England. By his time, the mid-seventeenth century, doctors were still using herbs, but were trying to be more 'scientific' about medicine, and they did not put so much faith in the stars and the movement of the planets.

28

The Doctrine of Signatures

There was another way of selecting plants as cures. Doctors studied the appearance of each plant and also noted where it grew. The appearance and the general habits of the plant they called the plant's 'signature'. So the Doctrine of Signatures grew up, which matched a plant's signature to its healing properties. For example, the wild pansy, with its heart-shaped leaves, was used as a tonic for people with weak hearts. A country name for the pansy is 'heart's-ease'. Plants with kidney-shaped leaves tended to be used for kidney disorders. Spotted leaves were made into drinks to cure acne and other spots and boils on the skin. Flame-coloured flowers were thought best to soothe inflammation.

heart's-ease

Plants which grew in damp places were used for the cure of diseases caused by damp conditions. So willow bark was used as a cure for rheumatism, a disease which can be caused by dampness. In fact, extracts of willow bark are still used to relieve some kinds of rheumatism. It contains salica, which was at one time an important ingredient in medicines used to treat rheumatic fever.

Plant Facts and Fancies

The Dangers of Root Gathering

The root was a very important part of many plants which were gathered for their medicinal value. In the time of the Ancient Greeks, there were men who earned their living by gathering roots for doctors. They were called rhizotomoi, or root-gatherers. In order to protect their profession, and discourage amateurs from going into their business, they made up tales which emphasized the difficulties and dangers of a root-gatherer's life. Peony roots, they said, had to be dug at night. If they were collected during the day, woodpeckers would come and attack the digger's eyes. When digging certain roots, you had to stand well to windward, or your body would swell up.

The most difficult root of all to dig up was the mandrake, which would shriek with pain as it was drawn from the soil. The mandrake root is supposed to resemble a man. It divides into two, like a pair of legs, and the swollen top of the root looks like a head. It is topped with a rosette of leaves which grow above ground at soil level and they represent the hair.

The root is very brittle, so it is difficult to dig it out of the ground in one piece, yet it must come out whole if its magical properties are to work. Altogether, collecting a mandrake was fraught with danger. At worst, a man who lifted one of these roots from the ground would die. At best, he was likely to go insane when he heard it shriek. The only way to overcome the problem was for the root-digger to arrange its removal without actually drawing it from the ground himself. So he took a dog along with him. After the soil had been loosened with extreme care, the dog was tied to the root and did the actual pulling, and it would die instead of the man.

Once the mandrake was out of the ground, great caution was still needed. The man had to take a sword or a sharp knife and draw three circles round the mandrake. When he cut it, he had to dance round it singing incantations.

30

a mandrake

The mandrake is thought to have been the earliest form of anaesthetic. It was the basis of the 'death wine' the Romans gave to those who were to be crucified to help them bear the pain more easily. It was also a plant of good fortune. A mandrake brought into the house had to be left untouched for three days. After this, it could be placed in a basin of warm water. This water was afterwards used to sprinkle the house and people's possessions in order to bring good luck to the house. The mandrake, in the meantime, was dried and laid aside in a silk cloth. It was taken out several times a year to be placed in water so that the house could be sprinkled for luck. The mandrake was also used in love potions.

Everyone wanted a mandrake and, in the end, almost any forked root used to be dug up and sold as mandrake root without anyone being the wiser.

Modern Medicine

In most branches of modern medicine, herbs are no longer used, but chemical properties of many of the plants formerly used by herbalists have been isolated by scientists and are manufactured artificially, and used in drugs. For example, herbalists used foxglove leaves, which contain digitalis, to relieve heart disease. Doctors no longer collect foxglove leaves, but laboratory-produced digitalis is used in the treatment of some heart conditions. Nearly 2000 years ago, the Roman writer Pliny the Elder recommended mistletoe juice as a cure for cancer. There is, unfortunately, no known cure for all forms of cancer, but in laboratory experiments mistletoe juice has been found to reduce some forms of it. If doctors decided to use this on a large scale, they would not have to go out (as herbalists did in the old days) to collect their own mistletoe. A chemical containing the vital properties of mistletoe juice would be manufactured instead.

Some people think that cures offered by modern medicine can be dangerous. A drug which cures one disease can, at the same time, produce serious side-effects which damage other parts of the body, and because of this, they are returning to the remedies used by herbalists in the past. Herbal remedies are slower to act, but they are gentler and do not seem to harm the system in the way that some modern drugs do. On the other hand, a herbal concoction will not stop an outbreak of cholera as swiftly and dramatically as modern antibiotics. The two sorts of medicine can, and do, exist side by side.

Today, doctors prefer to practice preventative medicine. That is, they hope to help us live healthy lives, so that we don't become ill as often as our ancestors did. One way to lead healthy lives is to eat the sort of food which does not harm us. A health-giving diet includes fresh fruit and vegetables, which provide our bodies with natural fibre and essential vitamins. It is perhaps in this aspect of preventative medicine and healthy living that plants are most useful to us today.

Now, just one word of warning. Never eat or drink medicines or tablets prescribed by a doctor unless they are given to you by an adult who is responsible for you. In the same way, you must not try to make herbal medicines, or eat roots, leaves or berries from the garden or hedgerows. Many of these things are highly poisonous. Herbal doctors use the minutest quantities and mix them with many other ingredients when making their medicines. If you want to eat wayside fruit, stick to blackberries, bilberries and wild strawberries.

4

Flowers in History

Flower Emblems of the British Isles

In the Middle Ages it was the custom for the nobility to adopt flower emblems, which appeared on their flags and shields and were embroidered on to the clothes of their servants and men-at-arms. In 1236, Henry III of England married a French princess, Eleanor of Provence. Her emblem was a white rose. Henry and Eleanor had a son who later became Edward I of England, and he inherited the white rose emblem from his mother. He liked it so much that when he came to the throne in 1272, he ordered that the white rose of Provence should be included in the design of the Great Seal of State which was used to seal all royal documents. Edward's descendants were the Dukes of York and the white rose became known as the White Rose of York.

Edward's younger brother Edmund was created the first Earl of Lancaster by his father Henry III in 1267. In those days, a great deal of France belonged to England and was ruled over by the English kings. Henry sent Edmund to France to put down a rising in the province of Champagne, and he brought back a beautiful red rose, which was quite unknown to English gardeners. It had been brought to France by the Comte de Brie, who had discovered it while fighting in the Crusades. Edmund liked the rose better than his brother's white one, and adopted it as his emblem. This was known as the Red Rose of Lancaster.

34

About two centuries later, the Houses of York and Lancaster became rivals for the English throne. For the next thirty years, on and off, the Houses fought against each other and the feud became known as the Wars of the Roses.

In Shakespeare's *Henry VI Part One*, there is a scene where Richard Plantagenet (later to become Duke of York) picks a white rose from a bush in the Temple Gardens in London and invites all who side with him to choose a rose of the same colour. The Earl of Somerset defies him and picks a red rose, declaring his allegiance to the Lancastrian cause.

Plantagenet: *If he suppose that I have pleaded truth*
From off this briar pluck a white rose with me.
Somerset: *Let him that is no coward nor no flatterer,*
But dare maintain the party of the truth,
Pluck a red rose from off this thorn with me.

In the battles of the Wars of the Roses, the rose emblems were not very much in evidence. In those days there was no standing army, but the king could 'press' men, forcing them to become soldiers, for a foreign war. Private feuds were different; when two rival nobles fought with each other they had their own private armies. The soldiers wore the emblem of the nobleman whose followers they were, and these emblems were not always flowers. The Earl of Warwick's men, for example, would fight under their banner of the bear and the ragged staff.

The Wars of the Roses came to an end with the Battle of Bosworth in 1485, when Henry Tudor of the House of Lancaster defeated Richard III of the House of York. Henry Tudor became Henry VII and began the Tudor dynasty, which lasted until the death of Queen Elizabeth I in 1603.

Henry VII did his best to unite the two Houses by marrying Princess Elizabeth of York. He gave up his emblem, the red rose, and united the red and white roses to make one flower. It had an outer row of white petals and an inner row of red ones and became known as the Tudor Rose. It is the floral emblem of England.

a Tudor rose

Until 1911, the leek was the national emblem of Wales. The story of the leek goes back to St. David, the patron saint of Wales. He was a bishop who lived in the sixth century and was much loved by his people. When they were fighting to keep the Saxon invaders out of their country, David advised them to wear a leek in their hats to distinguish themselves from the enemy, and it is a Welsh tradition to wear a leek on St. David's day, which is 1st March. The Welsh Guards wear a green and white plume in their bearskin helmets and on St. David's day there is a special presentation ceremony, when the Welsh Guards are given a leek by a member of the Royal Family.

The daffodil was officially adopted as the national flower of Wales, in place of the leek, at the investiture of Edward, Prince of Wales, in 1911. (This is the ceremony when the heir to the throne is officially given the title 'Prince of Wales' by the reigning monarch, and it was begun by Edward I for his son in 1301.) The daffodil was probably chosen because the leek, being a vegetable, was considered unworthy of the occasion. However, many Welshmen prefer to keep to the old tradition and wear a leek on 1st March.

The Scottish flower emblem is the thistle. While Alexander III was king of Scotland in the mid-eleventh century, King Haakon of Norway came across the sea to conquer Scotland. At Largs, the Norwegian army crept up on the Scottish army at night to make a surprise attack. They marched barefoot so that they made no noise, but one attacker, a few yards from the Scottish camp, trod on a thistle and let out a yell of pain. The Scots woke up in time to defeat Haakon's forces. In memory of the event, they adopted the thistle as their emblem. Much later, in 1687, James II instituted the Most Ancient and Most Noble Order of the Thistle.

shamrock

The Irish shamrock or 'little clover' was once considered to be a charm against witches and mischievous fairies. In the fifth century, St. Patrick used its leaf to explain the mystery of the Holy Trinity, the idea of three Persons in one God. On St. Patrick's day, which is 17th March, shamrock is blessed in churches and bunches of it are worn by Irishmen all over the world.

Apart from national flower emblems, there are other plants connected with royalty. The broom plant, which has the Latin name *Planta Genista*, gave its name to the Plantagenet kings of England. Geoffrey of Anjou, the father of Henry II of England, used to wear a sprig of broom in his hat when he went into battle. This was in the early twelfth century and it was a common superstition of the time that both the flowers and the seed pods of the broom would bring luck and save the wearer from evil, witchcraft and magic. Henry followed his father's example and took to wearing a sprig of broom. When he became king in 1154, he was known as 'Henry Planta Genista' which eventually became Henry Plantagenet. The king passed this name down to his descendants.

The floral emblem of France is the *fleur de lys*, which is the yellow water iris or flag. The *fleur de lys* is of much greater antiquity than the French rose. It goes back to Clovis, who was king of the Franks in the sixth century. He and his men were fighting the Goths on the banks of the Rhine, near the city of Cologne. The Goths were very fierce fighters, and it looked as if Clovis was going to lose the battle. His army had been trapped in a bend in the river and there seemed no way out. They were waiting to put up one last desperate fight as the Goths closed in on them, when Clovis noticed something which gave him renewed hope. He saw that the yellow irises which grew along the banks of the river extended far out into the river itself at the place where he and his men were trapped. Irises can only grow in shallow water, so Clovis realized that the river must be very shallow at the bend. Thanks to the yellow flowers, he had discovered a ford and he and his men were able to escape.

Another version of the story says that the Goths were encamped by the river while Clovis and his men were on the other side. Clovis discovered the presence of a ford by noticing how far the irises grew out into the water from each bank. He led his men across under cover of darkness, took the Goths by surprise, and won a great victory.

Whichever story one prefers, the result was the same; Clovis triumphed, and he took the yellow iris as his floral emblem. Much later, in 1147, when Louis VII of France went to fight in the Second Crusade against the Turks in the Holy Land, he remembered the story of Clovis and took the iris as his flower emblem. It became so closely connected with King Louis that it was called the *fleur de Lois*, or King Louis' flower. Over the years, the name changed to *fleur de luce* and then to *fleur de lys*.

Flowers in History

For years afterwards, all flowers in the iris family were called *fleur de luce*, until in the eighteenth century, the Swedish botanist Carl von Linne, better known nowadays as Linnaeus, began to classify plants. He used the Greek word 'iris', which means 'rainbow', as a family name.

Many of our large white daisies, both wild and cultivated, are known as marguerites. The French princess, Marguerite of Anjou, who became the wife of our Henry VI in the mid-fifteenth century, took the daisy as her emblem and had three daisies, or 'marguerites' as they soon came to be called, embroidered on the robes of her attendants.

Perhaps because of its new name, another Frenchwoman took the daisy as her emblem a hundred years later. She was Marguerite de Valois, who became Queen of Navarre. In 1587, when she came to Navarre for the first time, the townspeople greeted her with an enormous bouquet of marguerites.

Almost everybody has heard of Napoleon, but fewer know very much about his first wife, the Empress Josephine. They did not have a happy marriage, and towards the end of her life, Josephine lived alone at her home, the Château of Malmaison. Here she surrounded herself with a collection of beautiful flowers, and today Malmaison still possesses one of the finest rose gardens in the world. Josephine was very fond of her flowers and guarded them jealously. When she was given a dahlia plant which had come all the way from Mexico, where they grow wild, she tended it herself and collected its seeds. Over the years, the dahlias multiplied in her garden, but they were such great favourites that she would not allow anyone to take away their seeds or tubers.

One of the Malmaison gardeners was bribed by a Polish prince to steal a hundred plants. When the Empress discovered their loss, she was so angry that she had all the dahlias removed from her garden and refused to grow any more. The story does not say what happened to the gardener. Perhaps he went to work for the Polish prince.

Canterbury Bells are flowers which are called after the bells the horses wore on their harness when they carried pilgrims to Canterbury to visit the tomb of St. Thomas à Becket. Thomas had been a friend of Henry II, but after Henry made him Archbishop of Canterbury in 1163, he began to oppose Henry when he thought that the interests of the church demanded it. One day, in a fit of rage, Henry exclaimed, 'Will no man rid me of this turbulent priest?' Four knights of his court, thinking they were pleasing him, set out for Canterbury Cathedral and killed the Archbishop while he was saying Mass. Henry did penance for this cruel act and went to pray for forgiveness at his friend's tomb. Thomas was very quickly thought of as a saint and a martyr, and pilgrims set out on pilgrimages to Canterbury to pray at his shrine. The most famous story of one of these pilgrimages is told by Geoffrey Chaucer in his Prologue to the *Canterbury Tales*. The spot where Thomas was struck down is commemorated by a plaque in a side chapel in Canterbury Cathedral.

The botanical name for wallflower is *cheiranthus*, which is a longer version of an old word 'cheiry', meaning comfort. The legend about the wallflower concerns the Maid of Neidpath, the daughter of the Earl of March. He was very powerful and very ambitious, and he managed to betroth his daughter Elizabeth to the king of Scotland, Robert II, who came to the throne in 1371. Robert was a weak king, and many people feared that once he was married to Elizabeth, the Earl of March would become powerful enough to rule the country.

The earl knew all about the opposition to the marriage and was afraid that Elizabeth would be kidnapped before the wedding could take place. So he sent her for safety to his castle at Neidpath, on the River Tweed. While she was living there, Elizabeth fell in love with the son of a border chieftain, young Scott of Tushielaw. The earl was furious when he heard of it and Elizabeth was kept a prisoner in the castle and forbidden to see Scott again. He then pretended that he was going abroad, but he secretly remained in Scotland, disguised as a wandering minstrel.

One day, still in his disguise, he appeared beneath Elizabeth's window. He sang of two lovers, one of whom was a prisoner in her father's castle. He sang of how she escaped by climbing down a rope her lover threw to her one moonlight night. Elizabeth recognized the young man, and picking one of the yellow wallflowers growing on the castle walls, she threw it down to him to show that she understood.

A few nights later, when the moon was up, Scott returned to the castle with a rope. He threw it to Elizabeth, but in her haste, she didn't fasten the rope securely before she began to climb down. She was almost half-way to the ground when it gave way and she fell to her death in the courtyard below.

Scott was broken-hearted, but he went abroad, travelled all over Europe and became a famous minstrel. He always wore a sprig of yellow wallflower in memory of Elizabeth. In time, other minstrels copied him and the flowers were supposed to comfort them in their wanderings by reminding them of the sweethearts they had left at home.

Rosa Mundi is a very old and beautiful rose with irregularly striped pink and white petals. It is said to take its name from Rosamund, the daughter of Sir Walter Clifford, with whom Henry II of England had fallen in love before he became king in 1154. He married Eleanor of Aquitaine, the richest and most powerful woman in France, but he still loved Rosamund and they used to meet in secret at Woodstock Castle outside Oxford, where she lived.

Queen Eleanor found out about these meetings. One day, when Henry was expected at the castle, Eleanor bribed one of the servants to show her the way to Rosamund's room. When Rosamund realized it was the Queen who was coming, she ran away to hide herself in the castle maze. She had been doing

rosa mundi

some embroidery, and tucked the ball of silk in her pocket, but she had left her needle in the embroidery in its wooden frame. The thread stayed in the needle and unwound as she ran away, so the Queen had only to follow the trail of silk to discover where she was hiding. Eleanor forced Rosamund to drink poison.

Henry ordered Rosamund's body to be taken to the nunnery at Godstow. He had her coffin piled high with her favourite roses, the pink and white striped ones which she grew at Woodstock, and each year, on the anniversary of her death, he ordered that her grave should be covered with these roses.

A peppercorn is a very small seed from the pepper plant and one seed on its own is pretty well worthless. A 'peppercorn rent' is a token rent paid to a landlord who is not interested in the money, but who wants to receive some sort of payment, however small, to establish the fact that he is the legal owner of the property. In the past, 'rose rents' were frequently paid as a form of peppercorn rent.

Flowers in History

Perhaps the most famous rose rent was that which was paid by Sir Christopher Hatton, Queen Elizabeth's Lord Chancellor, to the Bishop of Ely. Sir Christopher was one of the Queen's favourites and she forced the Bishop to grant her Chancellor a twenty-one-year lease of the best part of his house and gardens. The annual rent was a red rose for the gatehouse and gardens, and ten pounds and ten loads of hay for the house. The Bishop was allowed to visit the gardens when he wished and had the right to gather twenty bushels of roses from them each year.

A rose rent of one red rose is handed over each Midsummer to the Lord Mayor of London by the Churchwarden of All Hallows. The ceremony takes place in the Mansion House and dates from 1346. In this year, a certain Sir Robert Knollys built a footbridge in the City of London without first obtaining permission. He was given a token fine which consisted of a rose rent for the use of his own bridge.

Another name for rose rent is 'quit rent', and until fairly recently there were quite a few examples of tenants paying rents of roses or floral garlands instead of small sums of money.

In 479 BC, the Greeks won a great victory over the Persian king Xerxes at Plataea. Before the battle, they had to lay their plans amid the strictest secrecy. They met in a bower of roses near the Temple of Athene, where they knew they would be undisturbed. From then onwards, the rose became a symbol of secrecy. In Christian times, roses were carved over the confessionals in churches to indicate that whatever was told to the priest in confession would be kept secret. Other places, particularly council chambers where kings and other important people met, had roses carved on their doors or incorporated in the carvings on the ceiling. This reminded people that whatever was said in these rooms was not to be repeated outside. In other words, things which were discussed *sub rosa*, or 'under the rose', were to be treated as confidential.

Linen is made from flax, but the flax had to be specially

cultivated and this made linen expensive. Only the rich wore fine linen and slept between linen sheets. So nettles were the poor man's flax. In Scotland people made nettle fibre and wove it into cloth. They slept between nettle sheets and covered their tables with nettle cloths. Nettles grew abundantly, and the poor country people could gather them free from any piece of waste ground.

The use of nettles as fibre goes back at least as far as the Bronze Age. Nettle cloth was found in a Danish Bronze Age grave wrapped round cremated human bones; the acid of the Danish bogs acts as a very good preservative. Even delicate things like fabric disintegrate only very slowly, so that scientists are still able to identify cloth fibres. In Denmark, like Scotland, nettles were used for centuries to make cloth and large tracts of waste ground were set aside for them.

In Hans Andersen's story *The Eleven Wild Swans*, Princess Elisa has to gather nettles to make the fibre to spin shirts for her eleven brothers to wear, in order that they may regain their human form.

The tea plant is a relative of the camellia and has grown in the east in India and China for centuries. According to an ancient legend, the fact that its leaves made a refreshing drink was discovered by accident. A Buddist monk was boiling water on a fire which he had kindled from branches of the tea plant. Some leaves fell into the water, and when the monk tasted it, he found that he much preferred this drink to plain boiled water. He passed on his newly found recipe and it proved to be very popular with everyone who tried it.

When the Dutch began trading with China and India in the seventeenth century, they bought tea among other things. By this time, tea leaves were sold dry, not fresh. The drink caught on in Europe and became immensely popular. A little later, tea was introduced into England and it became very fashionable to take tea with one's friends. The first Tea House where cups of

tea plant

tea could be bought was opened in London in 1657. The Houses became favourite meeting-places; it was like belonging to a club. A pound of tea cost about three or four pounds, so only rich people could afford to drink it. For many years, before the price of tea dropped, poor people would go to the back doors of great houses, beg or buy the used tea leaves, and pour boiling water on them to make their own tea.

A cup of tea is sometimes called a 'cup of cha', which was the name the ancient Chinese called the tea plant. In England, in the seventeenth and eighteenth centuries, tea was pronounced 'tay'.

In the sixteenth century, sailors set out from Portugal, Spain and England to open up trade routes round the world and to discover new lands. Sailing beyond the comparatively safe waters of the known world was as hazardous in those days as space travel is now. Probably in many ways it was more so. Today's astronauts are told when to sleep and when to wake up, they are provided with a carefully controlled diet and everything they do is monitored by experts on earth.

In those early days of exploration and discovery, the sailors had no one to advise them or help them choose the right sort of diet. One of the main problems of any long sea voyage was how to prevent a horrible disease called scurvy. It made their arms and legs swell, their skin flaked and their gums grew down over their teeth so that they could eat only with great difficulty. The disease was caused chiefly by a lack of vitamin C. Fresh fruit and vegetables provide us with this vitamin, but the sailors had to spend many months at sea, and they had no means of storing fresh food for so long. They had to live on dried salted meat, ship's biscuits, dried raisins and wine. When they put into port and were able to eat fresh food again, the disease disappeared. Those who had not been too badly affected on the voyage grew better, but others died from it.

For many years, no one connected fresh fruit and vegetables with the cure for scurvy, but they did find a plant whose juices helped cure the disease. It had a most unpleasant taste, so its juice was disguised as far as possible with flavours like saffron and spices. Because of its medicinal value, it became known as scurvy grass.

People on land were also liable to suffer from scurvy if their diet lacked vitamin C, and in the mid-seventeenth century, it became fashionable to take a drink of scurvy grass juice each morning. Some people even went so far as to eat scurvy grass sandwiches. Doctors made up a concoction of scurvy grass, watercress and oranges and sold it as a health drink. This was later replaced by lime juice, which tasted much pleasanter. It was the habit of drinking lime juice to ward off scurvy which led to English sailors and settlers in Australia being referred to as 'Limeys'. Many people still take a vitamin C drink at

scurvy grass

breakfast-time, but the orange juice we drink today is very different from the bitter scurvy grass of three hundred years ago.

Today, we think of big cars, expensive yachts, large houses or private aeroplanes as 'status symbols'. In Holland in the seventeenth century, the most important status symbol, incredible though it may seem, was the tulip bulb. The bulbs originally came from Turkey, where they were called *tulipan*. This is Turkish for 'turban', which the flower heads were supposed to resemble. By 1634, they had been introduced to Holland and were the most popular and sought-after flower in the whole of the country. Not only rich people but poor ones as well made tremendous sacrifices to buy tulip bulbs. With bulbs selling for the equivalent of £400 each, many were left penniless after purchasing only a few bulbs, and fortunes were made and lost in the tulip trade.

Bizarre tragedies occurred from time to time among the bulb merchants. One dealer bought a single specimen of a very rare and costly bulb for a vast sum of money, and faced poverty unless he was successful in raising it and propagating new bulbs in the years ahead. The day after he purchased the bulb, it was served to him with his dinner, in mistake for an onion. It was eaten before the error was discovered.

People set such a high value on their bulbs that elaborate precautions were taken to prevent anyone stealing them. Some enterprising herbalists concocted harmful potions which they advertised to put into the drink of anyone suspected of stealing tulips.

The craze came to Britain, but the prices never reached such astronomical heights as in Holland. All the same, bulbs sold for about fifteen to twenty pounds each in today's money. Tulip prices and the fortunes of the bulb dealers swung up and down for three centuries. In 1836, one bulb of the variety known as Citadel of Antwerp was sold in Holland for the present-day equivalent of £650. The mania had not quite died out in England either. In 1849, one English gardener got up on a frosty night to cover his outdoor bulbs with his own blanket. The tulips survived, but their owner died of pneumonia.

Primrose Day is still celebrated by some people on April 19th. The primrose was the favourite flower of one of England's most famous Prime Ministers, Benjamin Disraeli, who died in 1881. He was a great favourite of Queen Victoria. When he died, she sent a wreath of primroses from Osborne House, her home on the Isle of Wight, and a card in her own handwriting said, 'His favourite flower.'

Very soon after the death of Disraeli, the Conservatives founded the Primrose League in his memory and in memory of his political ideals. On 19th April, the anniversary of his death, his admirers used to wear primroses in their button holes.

Alexandra roses are sold to raise money for charity. It was on the 26th June, 1912 that the first ones were sold and this is claimed to be the first 'flag day' recorded in Britain. It was begun by Queen Alexandra, a Danish princess who married

Queen Victoria's eldest son before he became King Edward VII. In Denmark, as a young girl, Princess Alexandra had met an old priest who devoted his life to helping others. He was constantly in need of money and one day, when his funds had run out, he decided to sell the wild roses in his garden to raise the money he needed. Many people bought his roses and the project was a great success.

Much later, Queen Alexandra decided to do the same thing. She had artificial roses made in the style of the wild ones which had grown in the priest's house outside Copenhagen. She instituted Alexandra Rose Day and on 26th June she drove through London in a coach decorated with roses. The money raised from selling roses goes to a great many charities, and over the years many millions of pounds have been raised.

The Battle of Flanders was one of the decisive battles which helped end the First World War in 1918. Many men were killed that summer, and their bodies lay scattered in the fields where red poppies grew among the wheat. Many of those who were not killed, returned home badly wounded or crippled for life and both they and the wives and children of those who were killed needed help. So on 1st July 1921 a special organization called the British Legion was founded to do something for these people.

On 11th November of that same year, on the third anniversary of the signing of the Armistice, or peace treaty, over six million artificial 'Flanders' poppies were sold to raise money for the ex-servicemen's families. It was just an idea. Nobody knew whether it would work. But it was so successful that Flanders poppies have been sold on or around the 11th November ever since.

Today, the poppies are sold to help servicemen of both world wars, and the Sunday nearest to 11th November is kept as Remembrance Sunday. On that day, the Queen and members of her government and representatives of the armed forces and other organizations lay poppy wreaths at the foot of the Cenotaph, the national war memorial in Whitehall in London. In similar ceremonies all over Britain, men and women lay poppy wreaths at local war memorials. All these ceremonies take place at eleven o'clock in the morning, the hour the Armistice was signed in 1918.

The British Legion is now called the Royal British Legion and it holds a Festival of Remembrance in the Albert Hall every year on the eve of Remembrance Sunday. At the end of the ceremony, thousands of poppy petals flutter down from inside the building to fall on those standing below, while the Last Post is sounded.

5
The Story of Perfume

Perfumes made from flowers have been used for thousands of years. The ancient Egyptians were experts in the art of perfume-making, and Egyptian women kept their perfumed oils and ointments in beautifully carved pots and boxes made of alabaster. At banquets, slaves poured scented oils on the heads of the guests. The floors were strewn with fresh flowers and leaves, and fragrant garlands of flowers were hung all round the walls.

Roses have been treasured all over the world, for both their fragrance and their beauty. We think that the Persians were the first people to prepare rose-water. They boiled fresh petals in a closed pot and directed the vapour into another container which stood in running water so that the vapour cooled quickly and turned into fragrant rose-water. This method is known as distilling.

Crusaders returning to Europe from the Near East in the eleventh century brought rose-water home as presents for their wives, sweethearts and daughters, who used it to bathe their faces. It was also used at table in finger-bowls so that people could wash their fingers as they ate. In the days when fingers were used instead of forks, this was very necessary!

The Persians and Egyptians made a liquid which they called oil of roses by packing freshly gathered petals into containers filled with oil of sesame. The mixture was allowed to stand until the oil had absorbed the fragrance of the petals. People used it to perfume their bodies. Many thousands of petals were needed for these operations and acres of roses were grown.

Henry VIII had his own favourite perfume, which was a concoction of rose-water and oil of roses mixed with tiny quantities of musk and ambergris. In Tudor times, men as well as women used a lot of perfume. It covered up the unpleasant smells caused by lack of drainage and the fact that nobody washed or changed their clothes very often.

In the seventeenth century, in preparation for his wedding day, Jehan Gir, the Mogul Emperor of India, had a pool made in his garden which was filled with rose-water. On the day of the wedding, he and his bride the Princess Nur Jehan were rowed over the water in a small boat. They noticed a scum which was forming on top of the water. Jehan Gir scooped some of it up and found that it was thick and oily and had an exquisite perfume. Thousands of rose petals had been put to float on top of the rose-water, and it was presumably this combination which produced the oily liquid. Nur Jehan named it 'Atar Jehangiri' meaning the perfume of Jehan Gir.

We call it attar of roses and it looks rather like translucent butter. It is sometimes pink or brown, but it is more often green or yellow. Many roses are needed to make a tiny quantity; it takes about sixty thousand flowers to yield twenty-five grammes.

In France in the Middle Ages, peasant families grew and distilled their own lavender. Each family had its own still, and they made lavender-water in much the same way as the Persians had produced rose-water some centuries before. Later, professional distillers would bring their travelling stills round to the villages, and set them up in the market-places. People from all round would bring their lavender and it became a very friendly gathering as families waited their turn to use the still. The custom died out during the First World War, and afterwards it was replaced by mass production of lavender-water in commercial distilleries. The same thing has happened to the rose-water industry.

The Story of Perfume

The French region of Grasse in the Maritime Alps is famous for its perfumes, because the climate is ideal for the growing of lavender, violets, jonquils and jasmine. White jasmine is in special demand because it forms the basis of most perfumes.

Jasmine perfume is extracted by a process known as *enfleurage*. Sheets of glass are covered with light films of oil, and freshly gathered flowers are spread over them. They are allowed to stand for a day or so, then the old flowers are replaced by fresh ones. The process is repeated until the oil has completely absorbed the fragrance of the jasmine.

At the present time, Grasse has lost much of its old jasmine industry. The process is far too costly and time-consuming to be practical. Each jasmine petal has to be placed separately on the oiled surface and every petal has to be turned by hand every day. The industry has moved to Egypt where labour at the moment is cheaper and more plentiful. Hand-made perfume is very expensive to buy, and many perfumes sold in shops today are artificial ones which are made in laboratories.

There is a story that at the end of the seventeenth century the Grand Duke of Tuscany paid his gardener so badly that he could not afford to marry his sweetheart. In 1699 the Grand Duke was given a special jasmine plant. It was a very rare and fragrant variety and he refused to allow it to be propagated. The gardener secretly took a tiny cutting from it and gave it to his sweetheart as a birthday present. He told her to plant it and gave her instructions about how to care for it. From this tiny cutting, she grew a beautiful plant. She was able to sell many cuttings from it for a very high price, and soon she had enough money for the two to get married on. At country weddings in Tuscany, brides still wear or carry a spray of jasmine in memory of the enterprising young couple.

Most violet perfumes are made by steeping the flowers in warm oil. Old flowers are replaced by fresh ones until the oil has absorbed all the fragrance. This process is called maceration.

Plant Facts and Fancies

One of the most frequently used oils in the perfume industry is oil of Neroli. It is made from steeping orange blossoms in oil and takes its name from an Italian princess who used the oil to perfume her gloves.

In the eighteenth century, an Italian named Giovanni Maria Farina went to live in Cologne. He was a perfume-maker and he decided to try to make a perfect toilet water that would appeal to everybody. He took orange-flower-water as his base and blended it with other perfumes until he was satisfied. The result was the famous toilet water known as Eau de Cologne. Today there are many variations of Farina's original recipe, but they all contain orange-water and oil of Neroli.

When St. Benedict founded his order of monks in 529, he made it part of their rule that each community should be self-supporting. During the Middle Ages many monasteries kept sheep and lived by selling wool. The present-day community of Benedictine monks on the Island of Caldy off the Pembrokeshire coast make their money in a different way. They have their own perfume business, and bottle and sell their own very fine perfumes, which have become famous throughout the world.

Perfumes require fixatives to make them retain their fragrance. The commonest are the scent glands of the musk deer and ambergris, which comes from the whale. Since the killing of whales is now restricted there is not much ambergris available. Nowadays many people do not like to think of animals being killed just to provide them with perfumes, so they prefer to buy those fixed with resin, a fixative which comes from plants. Certain firms specialize in perfumes and toiletries which have been made without any animal products.

Frankincense is one of the plant fixatives for perfumes, and another is labdanum. This is a substance secreted by the hairs on the leaves of certain roses which grow wild on the hillsides of Mediterranean countries. As sheep graze among the bushes, they collect the labdanum on their fleece. The shepherds used to comb this off and sell it to the local perfume-makers. In areas where there was no sheep-grazing, the roses were whipped with leather thongs and the labdanum which gathered on the thong was afterwards scraped off and sold.

a pomander

In former times, before houses were built with adequate plumbing and drainage, people used to carry scented articles about with them to overcome less pleasing smells. An orange stuck with cloves was a favourite with the Elizabethans. The orange was usually tied round with ribbon so that it was easy to carry. Sometimes it was placed in a pretty bag or a decorative metal container pierced with holes. These were called pomanders; the word comes from the French *pomme*, meaning apple. Oranges were often referred to as 'golden apples'. Other pomanders were made from herbs and spices placed in bags or metal boxes. They were the forerunners of the lavender bags and herb sachets of today.

Tussie mussies or tiny bouquets of flowers were also carried to ward off unpleasant smells. Both men and women used pomanders, but it was usually the lady who carried a tussie

a tussie mussie

mussie. These tiny posies of sweet-smelling flowers and aromatic leaves were much prized by the Victorians, who gave them to each other as presents. By this time, household smells were not so bad, so tussie mussies were made for the pleasure they gave rather than anything else. Many craft shops sell them today, and people buy them because they are so pleasing to look at and give a pleasant 'old-fashioned' perfume to a room.

6

Floral Customs and Seasonal Decorations

Having a Christmas tree was originally a German custom. The very first Christmas tree was probably the one set up in 1605 in Strasbourg, the capital of Alsace-Lorraine, which was then part of Germany. (It did not become French until 1681.) Christmas trees became popular throughout Germany and were introduced to England a little over two hundred years later by Prince Albert, who came from the German state of Saxe-Coburg. He decorated one for his wife, Queen Victoria, in 1840. The Queen was delighted with it, and from that time onwards it gained popularity in England, so that today it seems a very English tradition. Christmas trees are decorated with lights, streamers and coloured balls. The fairy which is often placed at the top probably represents an angel watching over the crib of Jesus at Bethlehem. A star sometimes replaces the fairy and this obviously recalls the star which led the Wise Men to the manger. The lights on the tree may represent Christ as the Light of the World. Some people hang presents on the tree or place them beneath it and these remind us of the presents brought to the Christ Child by the Wise Men on the Feast of the Epiphany, which is kept on 6th January.

After the Second World War in 1946, the people of Norway sent an enormous evergreen tree to Londoners to thank them for their hospitality to Norwegian servicemen during the war. The tree was set up in Trafalgar Square and lit with white lights. It was much appreciated by the British, and every Christmas since then, Norway has sent a tree to be erected in Trafalgar Square. It is one of the familiar sights of London during the Christmas season.

Evergreen plants like the holly and the ivy are symbols of eternal life because they keep their leaves and so appear never to die. The holly has always been the most important of the Christmas evergreens. As the old carol says:

> *The holly and the ivy*
> *When they are both full grown,*
> *Of all the trees that are in the wood,*
> *The holly bears the crown.*

People in pagan times used holly to keep witches away. They also believed in mischievous spirits who lived in the house and did spiteful things like turning the milk sour or letting the fire go out. A bunch of holly indoors would keep such spirits in order.

With the coming of Christianity, the Church encouraged people to forget these pagan beliefs, but as they were very attached to the idea of holly about the home, it was given Christian symbolism. Its red berries stood for Christ's blood and its white flowers for Mary's purity. Its prickly leaves stood for the crown of thorns and its bitter bark for Christ's crucifixion. Altogether, the holly was very acceptable as a Christian plant.

Ivy, because it too is an evergreen, has always been associated with holly and eternal life. But from time to time, it has become unpopular. It rampages over trees, sometimes taking them over and strangling them, so perhaps it is not surprising that it is not always regarded as a 'good' plant. At times when people felt suspicious of ivy, they used it to decorate only the outsides of their houses, and where churches were concerned, ivy was used only as far as the church porch . . . just in case. A carol dating from the time of Henry VI contrasts the holly and the ivy in this way:

Floral Customs and Seasonal Decorations

Holly stands in the hall;
Fair to behold;
Ivy stands without the door,
She is full sore a-cold.

a kissing bough

There is an age-old custom which allows a sweetheart to kiss his or her loved one without permission if they are both standing beneath a bough of mistletoe. These 'kissing boughs' were made and hung in the house at Christmas time. They were hoops garlanded with coloured ribbons and decorated with evergreen and mistletoe. The most ornate kissing boughs had apples and nuts hung from them. In some country places, a mistletoe bough was hung up in the house as the clock struck twelve at midnight on New Year's Eve. It would remain there for a whole year, bringing good luck and blessings to the house. The previous year's bough would be taken down and burnt.

The Feast of the Epiphany falls on 6th January each year, just twelve days after Christmas. It is the custom on this day to take down all our Christmas decorations, which now include lights, cards, Christmas tree and paper-chains. Twelfth Night is the traditional ending of the Christmas period and there is a superstition that to keep holly and mistletoe past this date brings bad luck. But at one time, people must have been able to enjoy their Christmas decorations right up to the 1st February, the eve of the Feast of Candlemas. In his poem 'Ceremony upon Candlemas Eve', the poet Robert Herrick wrote in the mid-seventeenth century:

> *Down with the rosemary and so*
> *Down with the bays and the mistletoe,*
> *Down with the holly, ivy, all*
> *Wherewith ye dressed the Christmas Hall,*
> *That so the superstitious find*
> *Not one least branch there left behind,*
> *For look, how many leaves there be*
> *Neglected there, maids, trust to me,*
> *So many goblins you shall see.*

Herrick mentions rosemary as one of the decorations which must be taken down on Candlemas Eve. In both Tudor and Stuart times, rosemary was a very popular herb because of its aromatic perfume and because it was evergreen. Churches as well as private houses were decorated with it. A bunch of rosemary tied with a coloured ribbon and gilded made a New Year's present for a friend. It is a herb which signifies remembrance, so giving rosemary to a friend meant that you would not forget him.

There was a legend that after the Crucifixion, Joseph of Arimathea and the Apostle Philip left the Holy Land and travelled all through Europe preaching Christianity. When they arrived in England, nobody would listen to them. It was mid-winter, and Joseph stuck his staff into the ground while he raised both hands in prayer, asking God to send some sign to the people. When he had finished praying, he turned to take up his staff and found that it was rooted firmly in the ground, leaves were sprouting from it and, most miraculous of all, it was in flower. This amazing event was supposed to have taken place in Glastonbury in Somerset, and in the Middle Ages it was quite common to make a pilgrimage to Glastonbury to visit the Holy Thorn tree which had grown from Joseph's staff. Pilgrims usually took away a leaf or a twig as a memento.

The thorn continued to bloom each winter and it grew into a large tree which divided into two trunks. One of the trunks was destroyed in a gale in Elizabeth I's reign and the other was cut down by Cromwell's men during the Puritan rule in England. But that was not the end of the miraculous tree, for a few years later suckers appeared and the tree grew again. Seeds had also been saved and planted, and seedlings of the thorn appeared in many gardens throughout the country.

the Glastonbury thorn

Whatever the truth of the legend, there certainly is a thorn tree in the grounds of Glastonbury Abbey ruins. it looks like an ordinary hawthorn but each year it begins to flower and produce its leaves early in January, and so do all the other trees which came from the parent plant in Glastonbury. Before the calendar change in 1752 it often bloomed on Christmas Day; now it blooms eleven or twelve days later, round about Epiphany, 6th January.

Plant Facts and Fancies

In the small town of Appleton in Cheshire, a special ceremony takes place in July. People from the town dance round a hawthorn tree which is believed to have grown from one of the cuttings taken from the Glastonbury Thorn. There is a parade through the town and then the tree is decorated by children with flowers and ribbons. This ceremony is called 'Bawming the Thorn', bawming being an old Cheshire word meaning 'decorating'.

There are many legends and superstitions connected with May-Day Eve and May Day itself, especially about plants. The Irish believed that the sun rose especially early on May Day and that the flowers all opened extra early in consequence.

During the month of May, the fairies were supposed to play all sorts of pranks on the human race, like stealing the dairy produce which the farmer's wife had put aside to sell in the market. They were especially active on May-Day Eve, so people in some parts of the country protected themselves and their possessions by hanging up branches of rowan or mountain ash, which is supposed to keep out mischievous fairies and witches.

In other parts, people counted more on the hawthorn to bring them good luck and protection. It blooms in May and hawthorn blossom is often called may, though strictly speaking only the Midland hawthorn and not the common hawthorn is may. Its pink and white flowers are everywhere in the hedgerows the length and breadth of the countryside during the month of May.

Hawthorn garlands used to be hung in houses to protect them from evil. In England, this was part of the custom of 'going a-Maying', when the children and young people of each village used to rise before dawn to go out and collect may flowers, which they brought home in a sunrise procession, to weave into garlands. There are many poems, which describe this ceremony, one of the best-known being Robert Herrick's *Corinna's going a-Maying*.

Floral Customs and Seasonal Decorations

Come, my Corinna, come; and coming, mark
How each field turns a street, each street a park,
Made green and trimm'd with trees! See how
Devotion gives each house a bough
Or branch! Each porch, each door, ere this
An ark, a tabernacle is,
Made up of white-thorn neatly interwove.

The blossoms and greenery were interwoven into intricate shapes and designs while special songs were sung; this was all part of the magic. The blossoms had to be collected early while the dew was still on them, because dew possessed magical qualities too. The houses were decorated with may blossom and there was music, feasting and revelry all day. In the afternoon, one girl was to be chosen Queen of the May: a great honour.

The old rhyme 'Here we come gathering nuts in May' which sounds like nonsense, should probably be 'Here we come gathering knots of May'. 'Knots' means 'bunches of flowers', which makes much more sense. This is just the sort of thing the children would have sung as they came home with their garlands and bouquets of may blossoms.

In spite of that very old and happy custom, another tradition has grown up which says that taking hawthorn blossom into the house will bring bad luck or even death to a member of the family. Almost everyone knows of the superstition, but no one knows where it comes from. People in Victorian England certainly believed in it, and even today only very strong-minded people take hawthorn blossom into their homes.

There is a charming French custom where friends send each other letters containing a lily of the valley on 1st May. It is a sign of friendship and goodwill, although it probably began as a religious custom. May is traditionally the month dedicated to the Virgin Mary, so this was probably a way of wishing one's friends a happy month of Mary.

Henry VI was murdered in the Wakefield Tower in the Tower of London on 21st May 1471. Every year, representatives from Eton and King's College Cambridge, both of which were founded by Henry VI, place lilies and red roses on the spot where he was killed. He was buried in St. George's Chapel in Windsor Castle, and lilies are laid on his tomb on that day.

May 29th is known as Oak Apple Day. It is the birthday of Charles II, who was born in 1630. It is also, appropriately, the day when he came back to England as king in 1660, after the Puritan rule. 'Royalists' who had always been on the king's side decorated their houses with branches and leaves of the oak tree. They chose the oak because this tree played an important part in saving the king's life after the Royalists had been defeated at the Battle of Worcester. After escaping from the battlefield, Charles hid from the Parliamentary soldiers who were looking for him in a huge oak tree at Boscobel, near Donington in Shropshire. Cromwell's soldiers passed right beneath the oak, but the foliage was so thick that they didn't see him.

There are special celebrations on Oak Apple Day at the Royal Hospital, Chelsea, home of the 'Chelsea Pensioners'. This famous institution was founded by Sir Stephen Fox with the approval and backing of Charles II. On 29th May, their royal patron's birthday, the statue of Charles II which stands in the grounds is decorated with oak leaves.

Statues and pictures of Bacchus the wine god showed him crowned with a garland of ivy leaves. Ivy was supposed to have the power to remove the effects of drinking too much wine. If a man drank more wine than was good for him, his friends would weave him a crown of ivy leaves to wear so that he should suffer no ill effects the next day. Some enterprising wood-turners made wine cups from ivy wood to encourage heavy drinkers to drink plenty in the belief that they could not get drunk. Inns and drinking booths at medieval country fairs used to be decorated with bunches or bushes of ivy to advertise the fact that wine was sold there. Of course, good wine needs no advertisement, hence perhaps the saying, 'A good wine needs no bush'.

In ancient Rome, military victories were celebrated by a triumphal march. The victorious general wore a laurel wreath and rode through the streets at the head of his army while cheering citizens threw flowers from the windows and roofs of houses along the route. This was a classical version of the modern 'ticker tape' procession in America today!

An old country superstition says that buildings which have house leeks growing on the roof will be preserved from fire and lightning. House leeks have nothing to do with the vegetable which is called leek. Their Latin name is *sempervivum tectorum* and many people call the plant 'sempervivum' to avoid confusion. It is a low-growing plant with thick, succulent leaves which hold moisture for a long time, and it is able to grow and thrive on the slate roofs of old farmhouses and cottages.

house leek

The origin of this superstition seems to be that in classical times this plant was sacred to the thunder-wielding god Zeus (the Romans called him Jupiter). Where this plant grew on a roof he would not allow the house to be struck by lightning. Householders who took this superstition seriously would beg some roots of sempervivum from their neighbours if the plant didn't grow on their roof of its own accord.

Well-dressing is a traditional Derbyshire custom which takes place on and around Ascension Day. There are various explanations for it. The Romans used to hold a yearly festival called Fontinalia, when the citizens of each town decorated their wells and fountains with flowers. It was their way of saying thank you to the gods who supplied them with water.

The Derbyshire custom, however, seems to be a Christian one, and is centred on the village of Tissington, where several wells are dressed each year. During the 'Black Death' in the thirteenth century, when thousands of people died of plague, Tissington escaped owing to the purity of its well water. Again, in the drought of 1615, which lasted for six months, the five wells of Tissington helped the village to survive, for they never failed. So the wells are dressed each year as a thank-offering. The villagers collect flowers, leaves, moss and stones and press them into beds of damp clay spread out on boards. They make up pictures illustrating scenes from the Bible, with texts in flowers above the pictures and intricate patterns in borders around both. These decorated boards are set up at each well and visitors come from all over the country to admire them.

A very big flower festival is held in the Channel Island of Jersey every year on the Thursday before August Bank Holiday. It takes the form of a carnival procession where the floats are decorated with thousands of flowers, arranged to resemble animals and buildings, or to form intricate and colourful patterns. The first of these flower festivals took place in 1902 to celebrate the coronation of Edward VII and Queen Alexandra. It was so popular that it became an annual event.

Some of the floats represent, in flowers, various events of the island's history. This always includes the Battle of Jersey of 1781, when the local soldiers joined the English troops garrisoned there to fight off an attack by the French. The carnival ends with a Battle of Flowers, when the people who have been riding in the floats throw the flowers at the crowds.

Harvest festivals are held in many parish churches throughout the country. Blessing the fruits of the harvest and thanking God for what He has provided is an old religious custom going back to the early days of the Church. The building is decorated with fruits, flowers and vegetables, which are generally distributed to elderly people in the district after the service.

Flower festivals too are often held, and the churches are beautifully decorated with flowers; the festival often lasts about a week and everyone is invited to come and enjoy the flowers.

On Mothers' Day, many churches organize a special family service where children bring gifts and bunches of flowers to be presented as a thank-you token to their mothers during the service.

7

Naming the Flowers

There are a little over two thousand wild flowers growing in the British Isles and about as many cultivated ones. Like you, they all have two names, their individual name and their family or surname. Unlike yours, their names are Greek or Latin; this is so that botanists and gardeners from different countries can be absolutely sure which plant they are talking about. But many of our flowers also have English names, which are very often nicknames like 'dark-eyed Susan' and 'bachelor's buttons'.

The official botanical names of plants were finally decided in the eighteenth century by a Swedish botanist called Carl von Linné. He is more usually called Linnaeus, because botanists Latinized his name in memory of the work he did on plant classification. Linnaeus put all similar plants into a *genus* and gave them what he called a 'generic' name (that is the plant's 'surname') Each plant is then distinguished from the others of the same genus by a 'specific name', (that is the plant's individual or 'forename'). For example, the generic name for heather is *erica*, but there are many kinds of heather, so we have *erica cinerea* which is Bell Heather, *erica tetralix* which is Cross-leaved Heather and so on. You will notice that in the botanical classification, the 'surname' comes first.

When a new flower is developed, its botanical name is fixed according to the rules laid down by Linnaeus, and then its English name is chosen by the person who grew it. So we have a twentieth century rose like 'Elizabeth of Glamis' named after the Queen Mother, and 'Shirley Poppy' named after the village in Surrey where the local vicar first grew these colourful members of the poppy family.

The naming of flowers goes back to the early days of the world; and gardeners ever since have been choosing and changing the names of their plants. 'Flower Christenings' were held in Elizabethan times. There was great enthusiasm for growing carnations and London growers used to meet in taverns to discuss the plants they had raised from seed the previous year. If you take a cutting from a plant, you get a replica of the parent plant, whereas if you collect and plant the seeds, as these men did, the chances are that the plant which grows from the seed will not be exactly like the parent, and sometimes the seeds produce unusual varieties of the original flowers. Much of the talk at these meetings was very serious, and concerned the business side of the industry. But afterwards the growers would get down to the actual flower christenings. They drank toasts to their new flowers and thought up names for the new varieties, like 'Ruffling Robin' and 'Lusty Gallant'. Long before they had finished, these flower christenings must have turned into very noisy and convivial gatherings!

'Sops in Wine' was a name given to the clove-scented carnations which used to grow in cottage gardens. The name refers to the Elizabethan custom of throwing the petals into flagons of beer and wine to give it a special aromatic tang.

Many wild flowers have different names, in different parts of the country. If you live in the country, it is fun to find out what your local flowers are called. For example, the yellow toadflax is called 'butter and eggs' in Derbyshire. In other parts of Britain it is called 'puppy dogs' mouths', 'bunny rabbits' mouths' or 'snapdragon'. All these names make sense. Have you ever pinched the sides of this flower and discovered how you can make its 'mouth' open and close? If you can't find any yellow toadflax, you can try the experiment on antirrhinum, which is the garden variety.

toadflax

The lacy white flowers of hedge parsley which grow all along the edges of country lanes in May and June are quite understandably called 'Queen Anne's lace'. But how do you account for the name given in several country districts to the bright yellow stonecrop which grows all over stone walls? It is called 'Welcome-home-husband-though-never-so-drunk'. Alison Uttley, in her book *The Swans Fly Over*, suggests that perhaps 'a wavering hand clutches the firm little tufts at the cottage door as the husband steadies himself'.

Rest harrow is a plant whose name is more easily explained. It has charming pink flowers and grows throughout the summer in most wayside places and fields. But farmers in the old days didn't find it very attractive in spite of its good looks. It has very long tough roots which used to stop the plough, so the

Naming the Flowers

Queen Anne's lace

farmer had to 'rest' his plough or harrow and cut through the tangled roots with a knife before he could go on. Today's modern ploughs of course find no difficulty in dealing with the rest harrow's roots (if the selective weed-killers have left any of the plant behind to be dealt with!).

Bachelor's buttons is the English name of *ranunculus acris flore-pleno*, but the same name is used for about twenty different flowers in different areas. The one thing they seem to have in common is that they are all neat flowers which would make attractive buttons. A bachelor wanting to find a sweetheart would always have to dress well and his velvet jackets and embroidered waistcoats would be fastened with neat but striking-looking buttons. So the bright blue periwinkle is a candidate for the name. So are the marsh marigold, buttercup, scabious, stitchwort, tansy, feverfew, cornflower and red campion. All these flowers would make excellent models for buttons. In fact, John Gerard wrote in his *Herbal*, which was

71

bachelor's buttons (*ranunculus acris flore-pleno*)

published in 1633, that the large garden variety of red campion was very like the 'jagged cloth buttons' which used to be worn in earlier days. There is something special about any flower which is a bachelor's button – it has to be carried in the pocket and if it fades, it is a sign that your loved one no longer loves you.

Have you ever wondered why there are so many 'dog' plants? We have dog rose, dog violet and dog's mercury, to mention only three. 'Dog' means that they were regarded as inferior plants. For instance, the dog violet is not scented like the sweet violet which is grown in gardens, and the dog rose is neither so scented nor as showy as garden varieties. Dog's mercury was a plant which grew wild in the woods and was used by poor people for medicinal purposes in the seventeenth century. Physicians despised it and used the annual or French mercury which was grown specially for the purpose. To talk about a 'dog flower' is like calling schoolboy Latin 'dog Latin'.

Legends of the Flowers

There are some stories which are not true but are interesting enough to make us wish they were.

'Bedstraw' used to mean straw or any dry plant which was

used to stuff a mattress. A medieval legend tells us that it was on a bed of bracken and the plant we now call bedstraw that Mary slept in the stable on the first Christmas night. The bracken refused to acknowledge the divinity of the Child and so lost its flowers for ever, but the bedstraw welcomed him and its blossoms turned from white to gold.

Another version of the legend says that the bedstraw was left uneaten by the ox and the ass so that there would be something soft and fragrant for Mary to use as a mattress, and from then on it was known as 'Lady's Bedstraw'.

The Star of Bethlehem plant was given this name because its star-like flower reminded people of the star which led the shepherds and the Wise Men to the stable at Bethlehem. A French legend says that the Star of Bethlehem was one of the plants on which the Infant Jesus lay in the manger.

Pennyroyal is a low-growing mint which in Sicily is connected with Christmas celebrations. Children put sprigs of pennyroyal in their beds on Christmas Eve in memory of the belief that pennyroyal first bloomed when Christ was born.

A legend says that the Rose of Jericho sprang up overnight along the road from Palestine to Egypt, where it had never grown before, to mark a path for the Holy Family during their flight into Egypt, when Herod's soldiers were chasing them. Another story says that this flower bloomed at Christ's birth, closed at his crucifixion and opened again on Easter Day at his resurrection.

There is a tradition that the rosemary plant will never grow higher than the height Christ was when he lived on earth. When the plant is thirty-three years old, which was Christ's age when he died, it may perhaps continue to increase in breadth, but it will never grow any taller. The name rosemary comes from the Latin *rosa maris* or 'dew of the sea', but there is an old Spanish legend which links the plant with the Virgin Mary. When the Holy Family were on their way to Egypt, Mary did some washing and threw the clothes over a rosemary bush to dry. From that day onwards, its white flowers turned a beautiful blue.

The purple orchis has dark spots on its leaves; the tradition says that the plant was growing beneath Christ's cross on Calvary, and the marks were made by his blood falling on to the leaves. In Cheshire, the purple orchis is known as 'Gethsemane', which is the name of the garden where Jesus went to pray before he was crucified. St. Luke's Gospel, Chapter 22, verse 44, tells us that Christ sweated drops of blood as he prayed, so the Cheshire name must come from an old legend that the plant grew in the garden on the spot where Christ was praying.

Passion flower

The climbing plant of the Passion flower was introduced to Britain from Brazil in 1699. In each of its blooms we can imagine that we see all the details of Christ's crucifixion. Above the petals is a crown, which represents the crown of thorns. The three styles are the nails, the five stamens are the five wounds, and the ovary is the sponge which was soaked in vinegar. The ten sepals and petals represent the ten faithful apostles. The two 'unfaithful' ones are Judas Iscariot, who betrayed Christ, and Peter, who denied him three times at the trial. The outer corona of the plant represent all the other friends of Jesus who were at his crucifixion.

According to the legend, there is an angel who has the task of sprinkling the flowers with dew. He slept one hot day beneath a rose bush and when night came, he thanked the bush for its shade and sweetly scented flowers, and asked what gift it would like in return for its shelter. The rose bush asked for some extra attraction which would distinguish it from all other rose bushes. So the angel gave its buds the 'moss' which all moss roses now have and which makes them quite different from other roses in the garden.

Some flower legends tell us how people imagined certain flowers appeared on earth. Many are classical tales from Greece and Rome and some are Christian legends. Others, like the stories of the Guernsey lily, are fairy tales, while the story of the Forget-me-not sounds like a medieval legend.

A knight was walking along the banks of the River Danube with his lady. She saw some beautiful blue flowers growing on an island in the middle of the river and said that she wished she could have them. The knight, thinking only of pleasing his lady, rather foolishly plunged into the water to get them to her, still wearing his armour. He managed to reach the flowers and pick her a bunch, but before he could regain the bank, he was swept away by the current and the weight of his armour dragged him down. As he sank, he threw the flowers to his lady on the bank, and his last words to her were 'Forget me not'. The girl kept the flowers for the rest of her life in memory of the man who died while trying to please her.

When Adam and Even were turned out of the Garden of Eden, the climate of the world changed from summer to winter. Eve was filled with despair and decided that she no longer wanted to go on living if the world was always going to be such a cold and bleak place. An angel took pity on her, and breathed on some of the falling snowflakes. Each one turned into a snowdrop, to show Adam and Eve that there would be an end to winter and that summer would come again.

Many years ago, the story says, St. Leonard fought a wicked dragon in the woods near Horsham in Sussex. The battle raged for three days and it was not until the fourth day that the dragon was finally overpowered by the saint. By the end of the fight, St. Leonard's wounds were bleeding freely, but wherever his blood had dripped on to the ground during that long battle, lilies of the valley had sprung up in the same place.

The name dandelion comes from the French *dent du lion* (lion's tooth), because the jagged leaves resemble lions' teeth. A legend about the origin of the flower tells of the 'little people' who had to take refuge when men appeared and began to live in the world. The dwarves and gnomes went to live underground and the elves decided to live above ground among the rocks. The fairies could think of nowhere to go. They loved the sunshine and longed to remain out in the open, in the fields where they had always danced and played, but they could not live openly as fairies, so they transformed themselves into bright yellow dandelions. They grew in places where the sun would always shine on them, and we can see them greeting the sun today when they open their petals wide in the sunlight. If you pick dandelions and put them indoors in a vase, they will close their petals, because they need sunshine to make them open.

The legend of the Guernsey lily also concerns the fairies, but there is a far more prosaic (and likely) explanation of its origins, as you will see. According to the legend, a fairy came to Guernsey one day and fell in love with a beautiful woman named Michelle de Garis. She too fell in love, but had to agree to go to Fairyland if she wanted to become the fairy's wife, leaving her parents and her island home. The fairy gave her a bulb which he told her to plant in the sand so that it would grow on the shore and her family would have something to remember her by. A few weeks after Michelle left, her sorrowful mother found a beautiful flower growing on the sand dunes near her home. Ever since then, the flower has been cultivated in Guernsey, and it is said that it will not produce such beautiful blooms anywhere else.

Guernsey lily

The Guernsey lily is the island's national flower and is the emblem of the Guernsey National Trust. On 22nd May 1981, the Guernsey Post Office issued an 18p stamp commemorating their national flower. The stamps were issued in sheets and the legend was printed in the margins or 'gutters' between the stamps.

Another (and probably more accurate!) account of the origin of the Guernsey lily concerns the Dutch East India Company in the seventeenth century. Many of the Company's ships used to bring home South African wild flowers and bulbs for gardeners and nurserymen to cultivate in Holland. In 1659, a Dutch merchant ship was wrecked off the Channel Islands and some bulbs were washed ashore on to the island of Guernsey. They were buried in the sand and remained unnoticed until they began to bloom. In the autumn, wonderful scarlet and pink flowers appeared. The climate of Guernsey obviously suited them and they flourished. Local gardeners collected the bulbs and cultivated them, and eventually began sending them with other flowers to the London markets. They were a great success and became known everywhere as the Guernsey lily, although nobody really knew where they had originally come from. It was not until the nineteenth century that a party of exploring naturalists found identical bulbs growing wild in South Africa. By means of some good botanical detective work, the story of the Guernsey lily was gradually pieced together.

Most classical legends about the origins of plants tell stories of nymphs and human beings who were changed into flowers and trees. The legend of the sunflower is the story of the nymph Clytie, who fell in love with Helios the sun god. But he was in love with the daughter of King Orchamus and took no notice of her. At last, Clytie told Orchamus that Helios was paying attentions to his daughter. As she expected, Orchamus was furious, because he did not approve of Helios, who had a reputation for being unfaithful. He ordered his daughter to be walled up and left to die rather than marry the sun god. Clytie thought that now her turn had come to attract the god's attention, but Helios was heart broken and when he found out that it had all happened because of Clytie, he was furiously angry with her. Clytie lay for nine days and nights on the ground, neither eating nor drinking. She didn't move at all except to turn her eyes to follow the sun as it travelled from east to west through the sky. The other gods took pity on her, and turned her into a sunflower whose face follows the course of the sun each day.

A handsome young man called Narcissus had been told that he would lead a happy life until he caught sight of his own face. He avoided all mirrors, but one day he leaned over a pool to take a drink of water and caught sight of his own reflection. He did not realize that he was seeing himself and fell in love with the beautiful face which seemed to be looking up at him from the depths of the pool. He remained there for days, unable to tear himself away from the lovely vision. Eventually, he just faded away, and from his wasted body grew the narcissus flower. The cup in the centre of each narcissus head is supposed to be there to hold the tears of the dead youth.

A young man called Demophon fell in love with a beautiful maiden called Phyllis, who loved him dearly in return. But in the end, Demophon was unfaithful, and married someone else. Phyllis died of a broken heart and the gods took pity on her and turned her into a beautiful almond tree. When Demophon heard what had happened, he threw his arms round the trunk of the tree and burst into tears and it was so happy at this sign of affection that it began to blossom. Now each spring the almond tree blossoms in memory of the happiness of Phyllis when Demophon wept over her.

Some classical legends say that violets are wood nymphs who were changed into flowers, but there is a better-known story about violets and Io, the daughter of Inachus, King of Argos. She was loved by Zeus, the king of the gods, and his jealous wife Hera turned her into a white heifer and set the hundred-eyed monster Argus to guard her. Zeus was powerless to help Io regain her human form, but he created sweet violets, which grew all over the hillsides and provided her with food. The story has a happy ending, because Io did eventually change back into her human shape. 'Io' in Greek means 'violet'.

The iris grows in such a variety of colours that it reminded the Greeks of the rainbow. So they called the flower after Iris, the rainbow goddess. One of her special tasks was to guide the souls of dead women into the next world. For this reason, Greeks often planted irises near to graves.

Another Greek legend says that iris flowers are Persephone's handmaids, who were turned into flowers as they followed her when she was carried off into the Underworld.

Plant Facts and Fancies

Venus, the goddess of love, had a mirror which made the face of anyone who looked into it appear much more beautiful than it really was. One day she dropped it, and it was picked up by a shepherd boy who was in love with a nymph. As soon as the shepherd caught sight of himself in the mirror, he became so transfixed with his own beauty that he spent all his time admiring his reflexion and forgot about the nymph whom he used to love. Cupid, the son of Venus, snatched the mirror away from him and broke it. He turned the fragments into the flower we call Venus' looking-glass. The seeds of this plant are oval in shape and light brown in colour, and are so highly polished that they resemble a looking glass. In the days when mirrors were not bright and clear as they are today, they must have looked very much like miniature looking-glasses.

8
Tree Lore

There are many legends about trees. Perhaps because they are so much larger than flowers and stand upright, trees seem to have near-human qualities. Some are seen as good and protective, while others are to be avoided. But there are more good trees than evil ones. Most trees seem to wish us well and be our friends.

For England the oak is something of a national emblem. In the past England was covered with oak forests which provided wood for our ships. 'Hearts of oak', the ships were called, and the men who sailed with them were said to have hearts of oak also. When Henry VIII was felling oaks to build up the British navy, he took care to see that new oak forests were planted to provide timber for ship-builders of the future. He little dreamed that three centuries later ships would be built of iron.

There are many superstitions about the oak tree. It was believed to be struck by lightning more often than other trees. Shakespeare's King Lear shouts defiance at the storm with its 'oak-cleaving thunderbolts'. Because of this superstition (which does not seem to be founded on fact), the oak tree was always linked with the gods of thunder, Zeus or Jupiter in Greek and Roman mythology, and Thor in Norse myths. When the Anglo-Saxon monk St. Boniface went to Germany to convert the heathen, he destroyed a sacred oak dedicated to Thor.

Oaks were also used by the Druids, who worshipped in sacred groves in Britain and on the continent. We know quite a lot about the Druids and their ceremonies from Roman writers. When the Romans eventually drove the last Druids out of Britain, they destroyed their sacred oak groves because they feared them and felt that they held some mysterious powers.

Closely associated with oaks and Druids was the mistletoe, which was regarded as a sacred and mysterious plant. It is a parasite, which means that it has to live on another plant. It does not root itself in the earth but grows high above the ground, embedded in the branches of a tree from which it takes its nourishment. Mistletoe grows mainly on apple trees, but sometimes also on the oak. When mistletoe was found on an oak tree, the Druids thought it was a sign that their god had favoured that particular tree, and such mistletoe played a special part in their rites. Only a priest could cut it, and the ceremony took place when there was a full moon. The priest would be robed in white, he used a gold sickle to cut the mistletoe from the oak, and a white cloth was held beneath the tree to catch it before it could reach the ground. The Druids believed that mistletoe, whose roots never settled in the soil, must never be allowed to touch the earth. After the ceremonial cutting, two white bulls were sacrificed to the god.

Many of the sacred oaks of the pagans became holy oaks in Christian times. Some of these were called Gospel oaks. These were trees which stood near parish boundaries. On the Wednesday before Ascension Day, the Church of England instituted a ceremonial walk round the boundaries of each parish. The Gospel was read beneath an oak and this was followed by a beating of the bounds. In this ceremony, the priest, churchwardens and other officials were accompanied by boys who beat the boundary stones with boughs as they went past. The poet Robert Herrick referred to this custom when he wrote:

> *Dearest, bury me*
> *Under that holy oke, or Gospel tree,*

Tree Lore

Where, though thou see'st not, thou may't think upon
Me, when you yearly go'st in Procession.

An old country custom connected with the oak tree was called Shick Shack. It took place on Oak Apple Day, 29th May, which is described in Chapter 6. A piece of oak on which an oak apple was growing, called the Shick Shack, was worn by villagers until mid-day. After twelve o'clock, the Shick Shack was changed for 'monkey powder', which were ash leaves. These had to be discarded before evening. Anyone found wearing the Shick Shack or monkey powder late in the day could be soundly beaten with nettles.

The Romans used to present a soldier who had saved the life of a fellow soldier on the battlefield with a garland of oak leaves.

Much folklore surrounds the ash tree. The Anglo Saxons made the shafts of their spears from ash wood, and the Old English word for spear is *aesc* (which is pronounced 'ash'). Ash is a very durable wood and it stood up to much knocking about in battle.

In folklore, the ash has always been considered a good and kindly tree which warded off evil influences. The Roman writer Pliny the Elder said that the ash tree would keep serpents away. Ash leaves were taken into houses to keep out snakes and were worn as a charm to protect the wearer from snake-bite. People also carried ash keys, or seeds, in their pockets as a safeguard against witches. Ash logs were burned in Ireland so that the ash from the fires could be sprinkled on the thresholds of houses to keep the devil out.

It was the custom to look for 'even ashes', which was an ash leaf with an even number of leaflets. If you held one in your hand, you would meet your true love before the end of the day.

According to country superstition the ash was a tree of healing. The Reverend Gilbert White, an eighteenth-century country clergyman from Selborne in Hampshire, describes in

ash leaf

his book *The Natural History of Selborne* how local people used to think they could cure children who suffered from a rupture. Pollarded ashes were split and held apart with wedges while the child was passed through naked. The tree was then plastered with loam and bound together. As the ash healed, so, it was claimed, did the child's rupture. The Reverend Gilbert White does not record any successful cures.

Lightning can strike an ash almost as often as an oak, according to country tradition, hence the rhyme:

> *Avoid an ash,*
> *It courts the flash.*

Traditions about the elder tree tend to contradict one another. Some say that they are good trees, others say that they bring bad luck. There is a tradition that Judas hanged himself on an elder tree. Shakespeare was familiar with the legend, and uses it to make a joke in *Love's Labour's Lost*:

> Holofernes: *Begin, sir, you are my elder.*
> Berowne: *Well followed: Judas was hanged on an elder.*

People who thought that the elder tree brought bad luck were probably influenced by the legend of Judas. There is a tradition, too, that you must not burn elder wood or you will see the devil in the fire.

On the other hand, there was a belief that if you carried a stick or branch of elder wood, you could count on it to protect you from evil. Certainly, as we saw in Chapter 2, the elder tree has always been looked upon as the gardener's friend.

In parts of Ireland the hazel tree was considered a tree of power. It protected people from evil spirits and a hazel nut carried in the pocket prevented rheumatism. A double nut, or loady nut as it was called, served all sorts of useful purposes, like curing a nagging toothache. If you met a witch and threw a loady nut at her, she would go away.

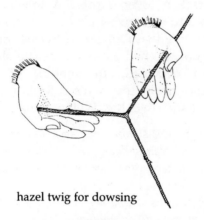

hazel twig for dowsing

A hazel twig made a divining rod for dowsers, that is, people who look for water beneath the earth's surface. A forked twig is held lightly in the hands with the ends poking out between the thumb and the index finger while the hands are held palm upwards. If there is water in the area, even if it is many feet below the surface, the hazel twig will dip towards it and the pieces held between your finger and thumb will twist and eventually spring out of your hands. Only certain people can do this, but it really does seem to work for some, though no one has been able to explain exactly why. 'Dowsing' usually means looking for water, but it is also possible to use the same method for detecting the presence of metal.

Plant Facts and Fancies

'Willows whiten, aspens quiver,' wrote Alfred Lord Tennyson in his poem *The Lady of Shalott*. There are several stories which explain why the aspen quivers. One legend says that the aspen was the only tree which would not bow its head as Christ passed by on his way to Calvary. From that time onwards, the tree has always trembled and quivered with shame. Another story says that Jesus was crucified on an aspen tree and as a result it feels itself accursed and different from all other trees.

The willow is associated with sadness, and a willow garland worn by a forsaken lover expressed loneliness and grief. Shakespeare uses the willow symbol in several of his plays. It was on a willow tree that Ophelia in *Hamlet* tried to hang the garland of flowers she had gathered, before she slipped into the water and drowned. In another of Shakespeare's tragedies, Othello, misled by Iago's cruel lies, rejects his wife Desdemona, and she sings the 'Willow Song':

> *The poor soul sat sighing by a sycamore tree,*
>   *Sing all a green willow;*
> *Her hand on her bosom, her head on her knee,*
>   *Sing willow, willow, willow;*
> *The fresh streams ran by her, and murmur'd her moans;*
>   *Sing willow, willow, willow:*
> *Her salt tears fell from her, and softened the stones;*
>   *Sing willow, willow, willow:*
> *Sing all a green willow must be my garland.*

Before the days of the mechanical cutter, hedges were trimmed by hand, and where a single hawthorn grew in a hedge the cutter would leave it alone. These trees were called 'lone thorns' and it was said that the fairies used to hang their clothes out to dry on them. If they were cut down, or used by humans to dry their own clothes, the fairies would be annoyed and punish the people who interfered with them.

Tree Lore

Yews were planted beside houses to give protection to the buildings and the people who lived in them, but they are also associated with graveyards. Most country churches have one or two yew trees growing beside them. Some people think that the trees were planted to protect the church from evil and to keep the devil and his evil spirits from disturbing the souls of the people who are buried in the graveyard. A more prosaic explanation is that the yew is one of the few trees which can thrive on the unpleasant secretions given off from the graves.

The yew has for centuries been considered a poisonous tree. The word 'toxic' means poisonous and we get that word from the yew tree which was called *taxus* in Latin. *Taxus* comes from the Greek word *toxon* meaning a bow, because the wood was used for making bows in classical times, long before it was made famous by Robin Hood. Its classical name, in the form of *toxicum*, came to mean all poisons. It has been suggested that yews were planted in churchyards because they are places where cattle and sheep rarely stray and so the animals were unlikely to eat them and poison themselves.

However, cattle and goats seem to be able to eat yew leaves without any ill effects, although they have proved fatal to humans and horses. Yew berries are not poisonous; birds eat them but humans would probably suffer from stomach disorders. To be on the safe side, it is probably best to keep both leaves and berries away from all live creatures, including humans.

The tree is most famous for its wood, which provided bows for the bowmen of England. A yew bow was made from the trunk of the tree, not the branch. The wood had to be straight and free from knots, so only a few bows could be made from one tree. Most of the bows used by English soldiers in the past may in fact have been made from continental wood, which was less knotted than the English trees.

There is a curious belief that before the death of a king all the bay trees in the country will wither. In Shakespeare's *Richard II* a captain reports to Lord Salisbury that:

Plant Facts and Fancies

'Tis thought the king is dead: we will not stay
The bay trees in our country are all withered.

Both bay and laurel leaves have been used to crown heroes. Successful Greek and Roman warriors were rewarded with a crown of laurel or bay leaves and in the Middle Ages, laurel crowns were bestowed on poets and artists who were sufficiently distinguished in their work. From this last custom, we derive our title 'poet laureate'. Chaucer in the fourteenth century and Spenser in the sixteenth were granted royal favour for their work as poets. Ben Jonson was probably the first regular court poet, holding the office in the reign of James I. The first time the actual title of poet laureate was conferred is thought to have been when John Dryden was appointed official court poet in 1668 by Charles II.

On Trafalgar Day, 21st October, wreaths of bay leaves are placed at the foot of Nelson's Column in Trafalgar Square in London and in a similar ceremony which is held aboard his flagship *Victory*, which is kept at Portsmouth.

As we saw in Chapter 6, the rowan or mountain ash is a tree which is believed to possess very powerful magic. People in pagan times had a very great respect for it, and the coming of Christianity could not break this tradition. On May-Day rowan branches used to be hung over doorways, barns, stables, sheep pens, outhouses and even over the baby's cradle as a form of protection against evil and mischievous spirits. Usually a branch of rowan was hung over the hearth as well to prevent the fire from getting out of hand, which it often did when there were so many fairies about! Better still, when the house was being built, the thoughtful builder would use a stout plank of rowan as a supporting beam over the fireplace. Farm implements such as yokes and ploughs were made from it so that the animals should be protected and the herdsman often used a rowan staff to keep his cattle in order. In the house, sticks of rowan wood were used to churn the butter and stir the cream so that they would not go sour in the making.

Another tradition about the rowan tree was that if you stepped inside a fairy ring of toadstools or dark green grass by mistake, you could prevent yourself from becoming trapped in it for a year and a day by placing a rowan stick inside the ring. The fairies could not resist its power and would have to let you go.

The idea that a tree has the power to protect us from fairies is pure fantasy – or is it? This book is about plant facts and fancies and it ought to be easy to decide which are the facts and which are the fancies. Scurvy grass and citrus fruits *do* cure scurvy and goat's beard *does* close its petals around mid-day. Those are facts.

On the other hand it is surely a fancy to say that the mandrake shrieks with pain when it is pulled out of the ground and that if a bachelor's button fades in a young man's pocket it is a sign that he is no longer loved. Yet there are people in several parts of the world today who are conducting experiments designed to prove that plants have 'feelings' and powers similar to humans and animals.

Maybe no two people's lists of what is fact and what is fancy in this book will be the same. While writing it, I haven't let you know exactly what I believe in myself!

Index

90

Index

Index